WELCOME TO HALEY STADIUM

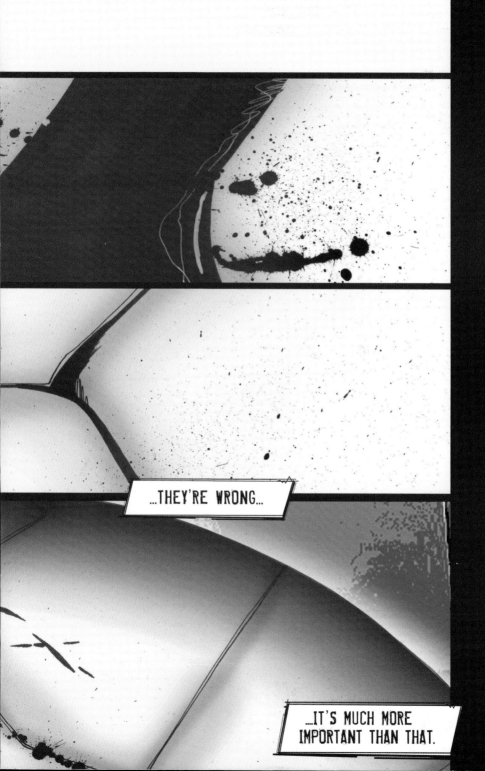

...THAT'S HOW IT ALL STARTS, WITH A DREAM.

...THE DREAM OF BEING THE BEST...

...THE LAST MINUTE TACKLE...

...AND IF YOU THINK DREAMS DON'T COME TRUE...

...WAIT UNTIL YOU TURN THE PAGE AND MEET...

...ZACK CASSIDY.

THE CARS. THE FASHIONS.

BUT JUST OUTSIDE...

TALK RUBBISH, MATE. HE JUST SCORED FROM THE HALFWAY LINE. PRESTON WAS A GOOD METRE IN HIS OWN HALF...

GRIZZ TWINRIVERS 13

HEIGHT	6'4"
WEIGHT	14 STONE
AGE	30
NATIONALITY	AMERICAN
POSITION	GOALKEEPER
WHEELS	HARLEY DAVIDSON #3

LAST SEASON

APPEARANCES	43	AGGRESSION	10
GOALS	4	CARDS	2 RED, 6 YELL
REACTION	8	PENALTY SAVES	93.4

SPECIALITY - POWER DIVE

12

KERCHING!
CASHBACK LADS!

YOU GOT CHANGE, MR TWINRIVERS? YOUR SHARE!

YOU GOT A JOB, BOY?

GARAGE AT THE WEEKENDS; I'M STILL AT SCHOOL.

THEN YOU KEEP IT SON. THINK I'LL GET BY.

HOW ABOUT A REAL ONE?

CHEEKY LITTLE...

WHAT?

DOUBLE OR NOTHING.

THE PENALTY KICK
WITH ALAN SHANE

"AS COMETS PENALTY TAKER, MY FIRST JOB IS TO SCORE. LOOKING GOOD COMES SECOND. I'LL SETTLE FOR A GOAL OVER A FLASHY MISS ANY DAY. THERE'S NO EXCUSE FOR NOT HITTING THE TARGET. UNLESS YOU REALLY KNOW THE KEEPER HAS A PREFERENCE, IGNORE HIM. YOU CAN TRY AND SECOND GUESS EACH OTHER ALL DAY. MOST TIMES I AIM FOR THE TOP OR THE BOTTOM CORNER - HARDEST PLACE FOR THEM TO GET."

OK ZACK, JUST PUT IT AWAY.

ACH!!

TAP

TRICKLE

THUMP!

19

GRRRRR...

OK ZACK - GET OUT OF THERE. NOW!

-GULP!-

GOOD KICK, SON. I OWE YOU CASH.

FORGET IT. JUST WANTED TO PLAY AGAINST YOU.

ALRIGHT LAD, THIS IS ALL VERY IMPRESSIVE, BUT WHAT DO YOU WANT?

ANDY "JOCK" COLQHOUN

HEIGHT	5'11"
WEIGHT	11 STONE
AGE	58
NATIONALITY	SCOTTISH
POSITION	I'M THE COACH YOU MUPPET
WHEELS	MORRIS MINOR

LAST SEASON

SMOKED	20 A DAY - BUT I'VE GIVEN UP NOW!
CARS CRASHED	2
SENT OFF FROM TOUCHLINE	1

SPECIALITY - SHOUTING

I WANT A TRIAL.

THAT SHUT ME UP, ZACK. STILL, I SUPPOSE IT COULD HAVE BEEN WORSE!

YEAH STAN, HE COULD HAVE FOLLOWED ME HOME LIKE HE DID PRESTON!

WORSE THAN BEING CHUCKED OUT BY SECURITY GUARDS?

ZACK, TELL ME WHAT THE COACH SAID AGAIN? BUT WITHOUT THE BAD LANGUAGE PLEASE.

DAD, IF YOU CUT OUT THE LANGUAGE THERE ISN'T MUCH LEFT, BUT THE GIST WAS "THERE ARE PROPER CHANNELS. NO SHORT CUTS SO DO IT THE PROPER WAY."

SUDDENLY...

HELLO TOBY.

YO DAD!

IT'S ONE OF THE LIVING DEAD!

WOW, IT'S LIKE, SPORT BILLY NO MATES AND HIS LITTLE SUBBUTEO PALS...

GOT A JOB YET?

JOB? WHOA, LIFE'S TOO SHORT FOR WORK, MAN. AND AT LEAST I AIN'T KIDDING MYSELF I'M GONNA BE SOMETHING I AIN'T, BALL BOY...

TOBY CASSIDY

HEIGHT	HARD TO TELL PERMANENTLY ASLEEP OR HUNCHED
WEIGHT	MORE THAN A CHICKEN, LESS THAN A CAR
AGE	19 BUT DON'T CATEGORISE ME, DUDE
NATIONALITY	ENGLISH BIRTH, JAMAICAN IN SPIRIT

LAST SEASON
WHAT ABOUT IT?

SPECIALITY - SLEEPING

MAKING IT
WITH LAWRIE McMENEMY

"ALRIGHT LADS. FIRST THINGS FIRST. IF YOU WANNA TAKE THE GAME TO THE PROFESSIONAL LEVEL, YOU'RE GONNA HAVE TO BE GOOD - ABLE TO PLAY FOR THE SCHOOL TEAM FOR A START. HELL, YOU GONNA HAVE TO BE BETTER THAN THE BEST IN YOUR SCHOOL TEAM. ZACK NEVER REALLY LIKED SCHOOLBOY FOOTBALL AT ST XAVIOUR'S, BUT HE'S GONNA HAVE TO START NOW."

23

ZACK! ONE-TWO!

THE ONE-TWO
WITH LUKE PRESTON

"MY JOB IS TO FIND THE PASS THAT CAN CUT A DEFENCE UP AND CREATE THE CHANCE. THESE DAYS, EVERYONE WANTS TO HOLD ONTO THE BALL AND DRIBBLE. IT'S GREAT TO WATCH, BUT THE ONE-TWO IS THE HEIGHT OF ONE TOUCH FOOTBALL. YOU PLAY IT TO ME AND WITH ONE TOUCH, I KNOCK IT BACK SO YOU CAN PICK IT UP. LEAVES 'EM WONDERING WHAT'S GOING ON WHILE YOU RUN FREE ONTO THE RETURNING BALL AND PUT IT AWAY. JUST LIKE ZACK AND ROBBIE..."

ROBBIE!

1 - 0 ST XAVIOUR'S!

BEING GOOD AT FOOTBALL HAS ITS PROS AND CONS - ON ONE HAND, ZACK WAS BECOMING PRETTY POPULAR...

COME ON ZACK!!

CASS-I-DY!
CASS-I-DY!
CASS-I-DY!

OOF!

...BUT ON THE OTHER, POPULAR PEOPLE ALWAYS HACK SOMEONE OFF, AND KIDS LACK THE RESTRAINT OF PROFESSIONALS...

ZACK CASSIDY 17

HEIGHT	5'7"
WEIGHT	11 STONE 6
AGE	15
NATIONALITY	HIGHGATE COMETS
POSITION	ALL OVER
WHEELS	BMX & SKATEBOARD

LAST SEASON - ST. XAVIOUR'S

APPEARANCES	26	AGGRESSION	6
GOALS	27	CARDS	0 RED, 3 YELL
GOAL PERCENTAGE	79	TACKLE	79

SPECIALITY   DRIBBLING, VOLLEY

LISTEN, CASSIDY, JUST BECAUSE YOU SCORED 5 AGAINST KIRKLEY HIGH ON FRIDAY, IT DOESN'T MEAN YOU'RE RONALDO OR ALAN SHANE, OK?

JUST SEE HOW YOU GET ON IN A SUNDAY LEAGUE TEAM...

THE SUNDAY LEAGUE

THERE. HE SAID IT.

THE SACRED WORDS.

THE SUNDAY LEAGUE.

THE HIGHLIGHT FOR MANY BOYS, AND A LOT OF MEN TOO. A GAME WITH REFEREES THAT AREN'T TEACHERS, WHICH MEANS-

A MORE "RELAXED" OBSERVING OF RULES-

YOU MAY END UP PLAYING BLOKES THAT LOOK LIKE THIS-

BUT YOU'LL BE MORE LIKELY TO PLAY FELLAS WHO LOOK LIKE THIS-

LATER, AT THE SKATEPARK...

27

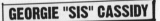

HE'S ALRIGHT. COME ON, WE'LL BE LATE. YOU SURE YOU DON'T WANT TO COME, DARLING?

IF ZACK'S PLAYING THAT'S ONE THING, BUT TO SEE THAT LOT RUN AROUND AND...

MUMS AND FOOTBALL

SHE'S GOING TO SAY 'SPIT'. TRUST ME, THAT'S THE BIT THEY HATE, FELLAS.

YOU WANT TO SEE REAL BLOODSHED, YOU SHOULD COME WITH US.

WHY? WHO ARE THEY PLAYING?

DAGENHAM DAMAGE, MUM. THEY'RE PLAYING THE DAMAGE.

DAGENHAM DAMAGE

THE 'DAMAGE' - HOME GROUND, 'THE KENNEL' - ARE MANAGED BY HARRY 'CUTTER' GRAY. A BULLDOZER OF A TEAM THAT ARE HAPPY TO GRIND YOU DOWN. THEY PUT PLENTY OF MEN BEHIND THE BALL THEN STEAMROLLER YOU ON THE COUNTER.

AND AS FOR THE PLAYERS? A PRISON TEAM REFUSED A FRIENDLY WITH THE DAMAGE 'COS THEY WERE AFRAID OF GETTING HURT.

AND IF YOU WANT TO SEE PROPER DAMAGE, YOU JUST MAKE US LATE FOR THE FIRST GAME OF THE SEASON. COME ON!

HALEY STADIUM

35

HIGHGATE COMETS FC

Founded:

1877 (entered league 1894)

Former names: London City FC

Nickname: The Comets

Ground Address: Comet Path, London

Ground Capacity: 71,105 (All seats)

Record attendance: 75,996 (24/1/51)

Pitch size: 114 x 75 yards

Colours: Red and Black (Home)

Telephone No: 020 778 667

Ticket information: (0870) 345 789

Fax Number: 020 712 346

General Information:

Car parking: Large car park at the ground

Other approved car parks are sign posted

Coach parking: By police direction

Nearest railway station: Highgate

Nearest bus station: St John's Road

Nearest tube: Highgate

Club Shop: At the ground. Open 10-4
weekdays. Match days 9 until 1 hour
after the match. Sundays 11-3.
Non match Saturdays 9-5

Tours: Can be arranged on main telephone no.

Ground Information:

Away Supporters' Entrances
and sections at North Turnstiles and
Chorley Lane Turnstiles.

Admission Info: (2004/05 prices)

Adult seating: £20- £26
(members)

Child Seating: £10 - £15
(members)

Programme: price £2.00

Disabled information:

Wheelchairs: 105 spaces in total for home
and away fans in front of the South stand

Helpers: One helper admitted per
disabled person

Prices: Free of charge for the disabled
and helpers

Disabled toilets: Located near the
disabled section. Commentaries are
available for the blind (bookings necessary).

www.highgatecomets.com

GAME OF THE DAY

HI, IT'S ABI AND GRAEME HERE WITH 3 OF THE COMETS' STARS...

CAPTAIN ALAN SHANE,

ROY "CHOPPER" DAVIS,

AND OF COURSE LUKE PRESTON.

IF I CAN START WITH YOU ALAN: WHICH OF THE DAGENHAM PLAYERS WILL YOU BE WATCHING OUT FOR?

PROBABLY THE ONES ON THE PITCH ABI.

HA HA!

HA HA!

OUTSIDE

I'M SURE I COULD WORK HIM OUT A BONUS PACKAGE.

GEORGINA!!!

LUKE PRESTON DRIVES THE NEW BEEMER SLICK

DRIVING THE NEW SLICK WON'T MAKE YOU LOOK LIKE LUKE PRESTON.

BUT IT WILL HELP YOU SCORE...

37

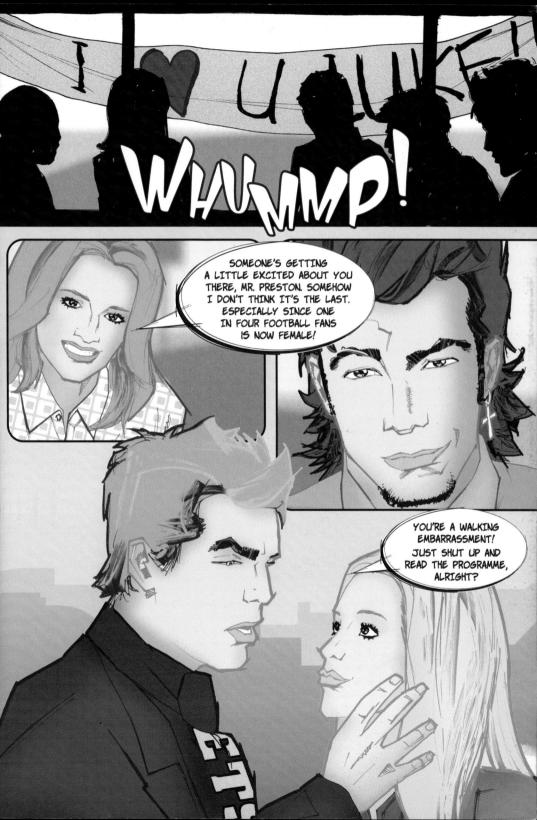

HIGHGATE COMETS
SATURDAY 15TH AUGUST

21 DI FLORES

9 SHANE

7 JOSHUA

10 PRESTON

8 SAMPILSON

4 JUILLET

17 FAKAMOTO

6 GOMO

5 DAVIS

2 MONK

13 TWINRIVERS

SUBSTITUTES: HEPWOOD, WEST, BATTS, McKINNON, THEOBALD.

HIGHGATE COMETS VS DAGENHAM DAMAGE

Ladies and Gentlemen, welcome back to Haley Stadium for the opening tie of the season between ourselves and our old friends, the **Dagenham Damage**. I'll be the first to put my hand up and say 'The Damage' aren't the best way to start your season. They've never been an easy game for us so it'll be good for the lads to roll their sleeves up and start as we mean to go on. It should also give you a cracking start to the season. I don't mind predicting now that the Damage will end up top six this year, maybe even winning a place in the super league – though Harry will kill me for saying that. Nevertheless, they are a fine club with tough and talented players, with more than enough quality and top flight experience – something that would have been obvious to those who saw our last Derby at the Kennel.

But we'll still beat 'em.

See, for some clubs, success is great. But for the Comets, success is compulsory... For the first time since I can remember, the injury level is almost non-existant. Our one worry, Italian hit-man **Massimo "Massy" Di Flores,** has come through his fitness test after his cruciate ligament surgery and starts today. Also, **Jeff Jones**, our fiery little Welsh defence dynamo is back in full training. Also in our favour, we have some great young players, like **Alan Shane's** son Jed, coming through the youth programme. And that's not to mention our midfield...

So many clubs lose so many games in the middle of the park. Not us. This season, there's no question of that. **Luke Preston** has settled into his central role, with French international **Marcel Juillet** proving more than a stand in for the recent departure (least said, soonest mended) of **Paul Swanders**. Whatever you may have heard, Paul left with my blessing and we all wish him the best. You can't blame a lad for wanting first team football, and the competition - with the arrival of Mr Preston - is just too much for some players.

I have every confidence that our boys are set to retain the title this season, especially if they continue to receive the support you gave them last season. We're in this together and if you continue to drive us on to bigger and better things the way a supporter should, who knows what might happen this year. There's more than one team that can win the treble... So, thank you in advance for your support and now let's get behind the lads and give Mr Gray's team a run for their money.

Enjoy the game.

Jim Carter
Manager

Jim Carter

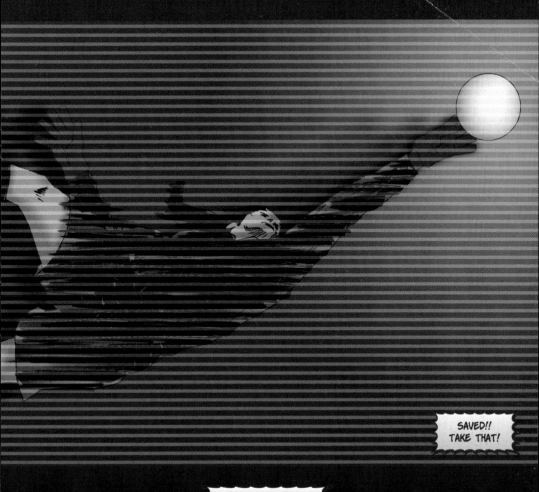

45

HALF TIME: COMETS 2 - DAMAGE 0
THAT'S HALF TIME - THE NOISE FROM THE COMETS FANS IN HERE IS AMAZING!!
ROAAAARRRR!!
COMETS! COMETS! COMETS! COMETS!
SORRY, WHAT WAS THAT TONY?!

64 MINUTES...

WES JOSHUA DOING WHAT HE DOES BEST – HE'S ALL OVER THE DEFENCE!

IT'S STILL JOSHUA...

ON TO DI FLORES...

GOALLLLLLL!!!

3-0

86 MINUTES...

IT'S SHANE...

TO JOSHUA...

TO PRESTON...

BACK TO SHANE...

SHANE'S FOUND SPACE!

SHANE 9

OH, IT'S A HOLLYWOOD PASS, AND...

IT'S **PRESTON!**

GOOOOOOAAAAAAAAALLLLLL!!!!!

4-0

HIGHGATE COMETS 4
DAGENHAM DAMAGE 0

I TELL YOU SON, YOU WATCH ALAN SHANE AND YOU'LL LEARN ALL YOU NEED TO KNOW ABOUT RUNNING OFF THE BALL AND PLAYING FOR THE TEAM... USE IT AT THE COUNTY TRIALS. COME ON, LET'S GO.

COME ON...   GET...   BACK...   ZACK...

NO GOALS FROM THE 'WONDER BOY' THEY TOLD ME ABOUT?

WOULD'VE HELPED IF I COULD HAVE GOT OUTTA OUR OWN HALF!

I KNOW, BUT YOU DID THE RIGHT THING. SEE YOU AT PRACTICE?

WHAT?... BUT WHAT ABOUT?

OUR ROCK STAR STRIKER? FORGET IT, HE'S SELFISH - THIS IS A TEAM GAME. YOU PROPPED US UP OUT THERE, CASSIDY. YOU PLAYED FOR THE TEAM AND SET UP OUR GOAL.

I'LL SEE YOU SATURDAY.

YESSSS!!

SUFFOLK COLTS VS GREATER LONDON BOYS

GOAL CELEBRATIONS
WITH WES JOSHUA

"THIS STUFF IS ALL IMPORTANT THESE DAYS SO LISTEN UP. THE GOAL GETS YOUR NAME ON THE SCORE SHEET. THAT'S COOL, BUT YOU GOTTA WIN THE CROWD, MAN. GET YOURSELF A TRADEMARK. YOU COULD USE THE FLYING PLANE, THE CLAIMING OF THE CORNER FLAG, THE SHIRT PULLED UP OVER THE FACE OR GET ACROBATIC. IF IT WORKS, USE IT, KNOW WHAT I MEAN? JUST DON'T FOLLOW MY BOY DUNCAN HERE... WHY? OK, TAKE A LOOK BUT DON'T SAY I DIDN'T WARN YOU, THAT BOY'S A 'TOON - A LOONEY TOON..."

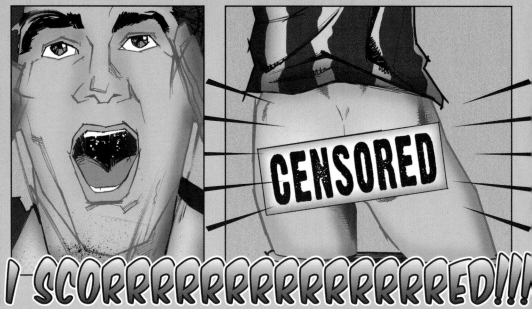

I SCORRRRRRRRRRRRRED!!!

YOU'VE GOT TO BE... MY MUM'S WATCHING!

IT DON'T STOP THERE...

THEN... BLAM! STRAIGHT IN!

SOUNDS SWEET. WISH I'D SEEN IT.

YOU DON'T - WE ALL SAW TOO MUCH THAT DAY. TRUST ME, MY MUM HASN'T BEEN THE SAME SINCE! WHOA! WHO'S THAT?!

DON'T EVEN THINK ABOUT IT. SHE'S GOING OUT WITH THOMPSON.

WHO?

THOMPSON

HEIGHT	REALLY TALL
WEIGHT	REALLY HEAVY
AGE	

LOOK, WE DON'T NEED THIS, HE CAN'T PLAY. ALL HE CAN DO IS HIT PEOPLE AND FEED HIS PET VIPER.

YES!

THAT'S ONE... THOUGHT WHERE YOU WANT TO GO YET?

YOU NEVER SAID ANYTHING ABOUT PENALTIES COUNTING. I WANT TWO GOALS IN OPEN PLAY, MATE.

SHE WANTS A HAT-TRICK!

HA HA PLAYSTATION, HERE YOU COME...

HOW HARD WOULD YOU TRY FOR THE HAT TRICK?

EXACTLY.

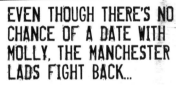

EVEN THOUGH THERE'S NO CHANCE OF A DATE WITH MOLLY, THE MANCHESTER LADS FIGHT BACK...

69

HELLO ZACK. I'M AUDY MCMAHON. CHIEF SCOUT FOR THE COMETS.

CHIEF SCOUT FOR..?

THE NEXT DAY...

REMEMBER SON, THIS IS A CHANCE IN A BILLION. TAKE IT.

THESE BOYS AREN'T LOOKING FOR JUGGLING OR THE FANCY STUFF. GOOD ONE-TOUCH FOOTBALL, SPACIAL AWARENESS AND SERIOUS WORK RATE, OK?

TEACH YOURSELF FOOTBALL

WHAT?!

IF YOU SEE PRESTON -

- TELL HIM YOU WERE THE BUNNY BOILER WITH THE BANNER, YEAH, OK. RIGHT, GOTTA GO.

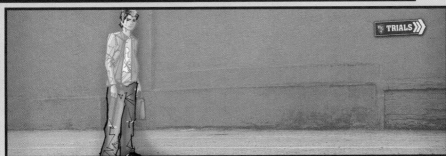

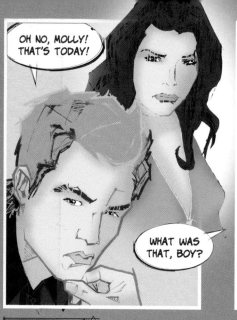

OH NO, MOLLY! THAT'S TODAY!

WHAT WAS THAT, BOY?

ERR... I JUST SNEEZED, GAFFER.

WELL, YOU'D BETTER PRAY I DON'T CATCH IT! LADS, THERE IS NO BETTE TIME TO BE A FOOTBALLE ANYONE PLAYING IN THE TC FLIGHT FOR A FEW SEASON WILL END UP A MILLIONAIRE BUT YOU'RE GONNA HAVE T EARN IT. RIGHT. ON YOUR FE LET'S SEE HOW FIT YOU AF

KICKABOUT...

80

25 MINS

32 MINS

39 MINS

50 MINS

77 MINS

81 MINS

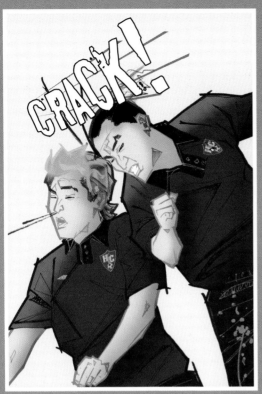

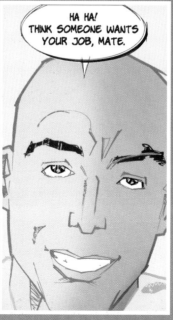

89

ZACK, GETTING AN AGENT TO REPRESENT YOU ISN'T THE PROBLEM. WE JUST NEED THE RIGHT ONE.

WELL I HOPE HE GETS A MOVE ON, THE PAPER'S COMING ROUND IN A MINUTE.

DING DONG!

AHA! HERE HE IS!

I CAN'T BELIEVE YOUR CHEEK. YOU STAND ME UP AND DON'T EVEN THINK TO GIVE ME A CALL?

OH! ERR, SORRY MOLLY... I HAD A TRIAL FOR THE...

95

OK, GENTLEMEN, OVER HERE...

AH, CASSIDY, WELCOME. YOU JOIN JUST IN TIME FOR A LITTLE CHAT.

THE LAST FEW MATCHES WE'VE WON. 1-0. NOW WINNING'S ONE THING, GREAT. BUT THE COMETS ARE NOT, REPEAT NOT, A 1-0 CLUB.

IF YOU MAKE IT TO THE FIRST TEAM, YOU'LL FIND YOU GET YOUR WIN BONUS, BUT INDIVIDUAL GOAL BONUSES DON'T KICK IN 'TIL WE HIT THE 2 GOAL MARK. THAT'S HOW SERIOUS WE ARE. OUR SUPPORTERS DESERVE BETTER THAN 1-0 AND IF YOU WANT TO STAY ON THE TEAM, YOU'D BETTER START THINKING THAT WAY.

CLEAR? OK, LECTURE OVER. LET'S PLAY SOME FOOTBALL.

15... 16... 17... YEAAAAYYYYYYYYY! HAPPY BIRTHDAY ZACK!

CAN YOU BELIEVE WE'RE HERE, DOING THIS? I'M TRAINING WITH THE COMETS ON MY BIRTHDAY...

IT'S NOT ALL GLAMOUR...

CAN YOU BELIEVE IT. I'M CLEANING THE CHANGING ROOM FLOOR ON MY BIRTHDAY...

ZACK, LOOK AT THESE, "THE WES JOSHUA HUNTER". D'YA RECKON WE'LL HAVE SOMETHING LIKE THIS ONE DAY?

TOO RIGHT! WE WILL.

W J HUNTER

LATER...

I'M JUST SAYING IT'S NOT A GOOD IDEA. WHILE YOU'RE IN THE YOUTH TEAM YOU SOCIALISE WITH THE YOUTH TEAM. OTHERWISE YOU LOOK LIKE A HOTSHOT. YOU HAVE TO EARN THE RIGHT TO TALK TO THE PLAYERS.

HEY WALLY!

HI ZACK

YOU SPOKE TO WALLY?

YEAH, HE HELPED ME FIND THE WAY HERE AT THE TRIALS. SOME GIT TURNED ALL THE SIGNS AROUND.

THAT WAS VASEY. WELL YOU COULD DO A LOT WORSE THAN TALK TO HIM. HE USED TO PLAY FOR THE COMETS BACK IN THE '40S AND '50S.

HANG ON BOSS. THE COMETS HAVE NEVER HAD ANYONE CALLED 'WALLY'.

111

113

THE BIG MAN COULDN'T DO ANYTHING ABOUT THAT ONE. COULD WE BE IN FOR AN UPSET HERE?

SNAP!!

AND YOUNG SHANE'S RESPONSIBLE. BOY'S SUFFERING FROM A BAD CASE OF NERVES TONIGHT, TONY.

50 MINUTES...

...AND WITH PRESTON OFF THE SQUAD DUE TO TEAM ROTATION, WES JOSHUA STEPS UP...

CLEARED BY WESTFIELD...

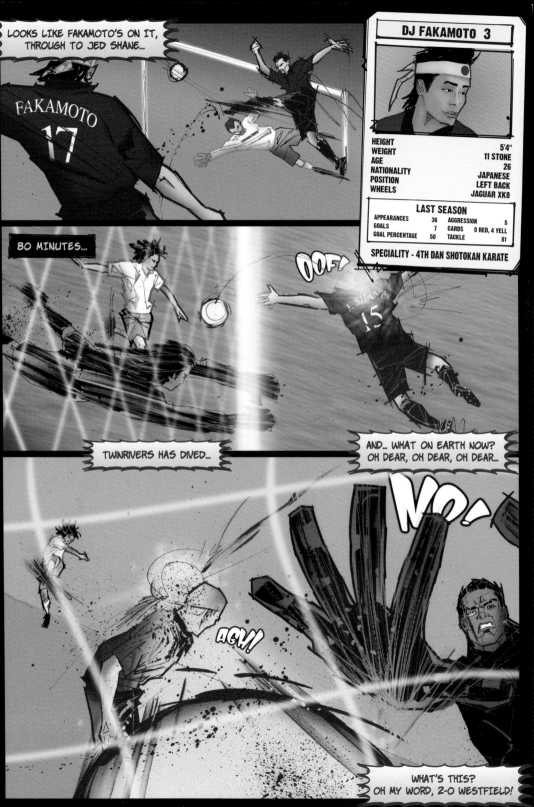

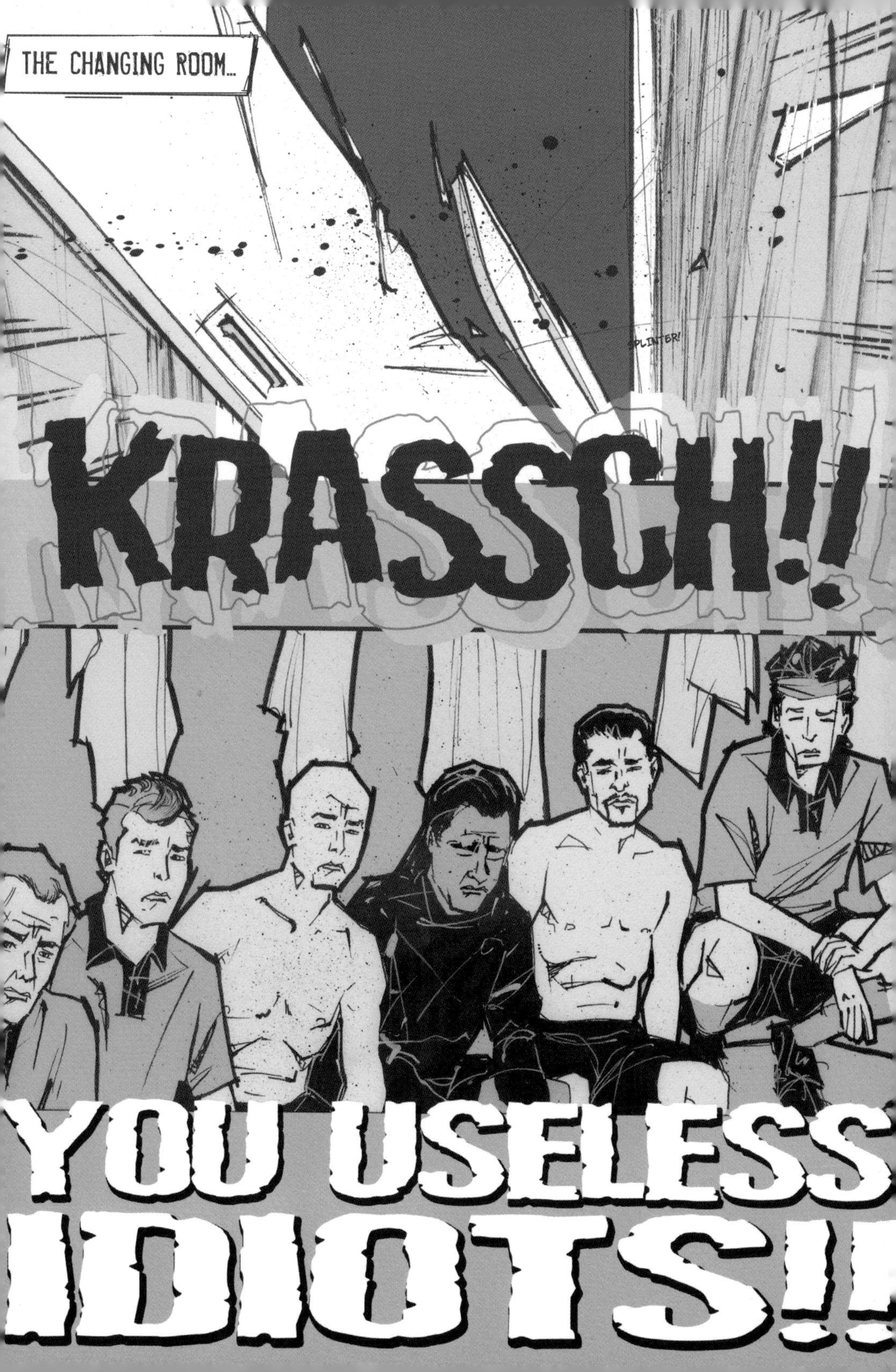
THE CHANGING ROOM...
KRASSCH!!
YOU USELESS
IDIOTS!!

SORRY TO CALL YOU IN SO LATE, ZACK, BUT I THOUGHT IT WAS ONLY FAIR TO TALK TO YOU IN PERSON.

SO, ER... FIRST, HOW'D THE DRIVING TEST GO?

I PASSED.

WELL DONE. I HOPE YOU HAVEN'T BOUGHT A CAR YET...

WHY? WHAT'S WRONG?

129

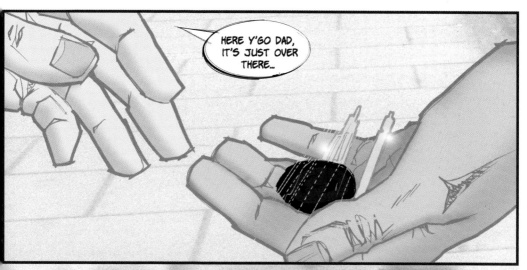

ZACK?

MAGNIFICO!

FLOODLIGHT TV

HI, COMET LOVERS EVERYWHERE. I'M GLORIA KINNEY AND IN THIS WEEK'S "FLOODLIGHT" WE'LL BE HAVING A LOOK AT ONE OF THE PLAYERS TIPPED FOR THE TOP AND CURRENTLY MAKING HIS NAME IN THE RESERVES WITH MASSY DI FLORES UP FRONT... ZACK CASSIDY.

FLOODLIGHT TV

AFTER ONLY 2 MONTHS IN THE RESERVES, RUMOURS ARE CIRCULATING OF YOUNG ZACK, STILL ONLY 17, MAKING IT TO THE FIRST TEAM SQUAD. WE COLLARED HIM AFTER THE COMETS' PASTING OF DERBY VILLA AT HOME.

SO, ZACK, IS IT TRUE THAT THE BOSS IS GOING TO GIVE YOU A TRY IN THE FIRST TEAM AGAINST THE ROVERS?

HELLO ROBBIE?

ZACK'S ON TV!!!

CHECK IT OUT...

FLOODLIGHT TV

AND MASSIMO, HOW DO YOU FEEL ABOUT HAVING ZACK SNAPPING AT YOUR HEELS?

HE'S A GOOD KID. I THINK ALAN AND JED SHANE ARE HOPING SOMEONE BUYS HIM QUICK, YES?

FLOODLIGHT TV

ARE YOU GONNA "MAKE HIM AN OFFER HE CAN'T REFUSE?"

FLOODLIGHT TV

THAT'S NOT FUNNY, GLORIA. MY FAMILY HAS NOTHING TO DO WITH THE MAFIA AND PEOPLE WHO SAY SUCH THINGS GET HURT. UNDERSTAND?

FLOODLIGHT TV

ERRR... YES, SORRY...

MAKING IT
WITH LAWRIE McMENEMY

"THERE'S NOTHING QUITE LIKE YOUR FIRST DAY TRAINING WITH THE FIRST TEAM..."

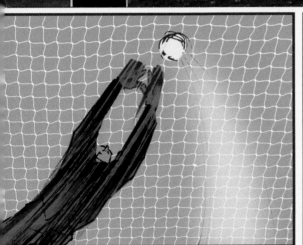

HUMPHH...

CASSIDY MIGHT DO, YOU KNOW. WANNA START HIM AT THE ROVERS?

I'LL THINK ABOUT IT.

...AND JED'S ASKED FOR MASSY'S NUMBER 11 SHIRT, BUT I'M NOT SURE.

HMMM, CHECK MASSY WITH THE SWEDE FIRST.

A FEW SHOPS LATER...

RIGHT, WELL WE'D BETTER GO NOW, MAN.

I'VE GOT ENOUGH NOW, OK?

WHERE NOW?

PHOTO SHOOT FOR ELEVEN MAGAZINE.

ELEVEN? YOU'RE KIDDING! OH WELL SEE YA!

WHAT'RE YOU TALKING ABOUT? YOU'RE COMING WITH US...

HOW DO YOU COPE? THIS IS CRAZY...

LISTEN MATE, THIS IS NOTHING. THEY DON'T EVEN KNOW WHO YOU ARE YET. ONCE THEY DO, YOU'RE GONNA FIND OUT A HELL OF A LOT...

ABOUT WHAT?

ABOUT YOURSELF. IF YOU'RE SMART, YOU'LL TAKE WHAT YOU NEED FROM EACH OF US...

...CHOPPER'S FIRE, GRIZZ'S STRENGTH, SHANE'S LEADERSHIP, WES' FLAIR, MASSY'S KILLER INSTINCT AND MY... ERM...

145

146

CLICK
CLICK
HIGHGAT
CLICK
COME
CLICK
CLICK
vandal
CLICK
CLICK
OH DARLINGS, THAT'S ABSOLUTELY WONDERFUL!

INTERVIEW:

IN THE SPOTLIGHT

ELEVEN MAGAZINE TALKS EXCLUSIVELY
TO LUKE PRESTON AND WES JOSHUA

At what age did you start playing football?

LP: I think I was about 6 when I joined the kids' after school club. Then I joined a local team that played on Saturday mornings; Pakefield United they were called.
WJ: Think my Dad threw a ball at me when I was 2. Mum says I wouldn't give it back.

Did you get a lot of support from your parents?

LP: Oh yes. My mum used to stand and watch on Saturday mornings, freezing to death on the touchline. It was tough for her 'cos when I started she didn't know a lot about football. She does now though!
WJ: Completely. Mum never moaned about washing my kit, whatever I did. The mums are the heroes, man.

LP

Did you always want to be a professional football player?

LP: Not at all, no. To be honest, when I was really young I wanted to be a fireman. I used to talk about it all the time. It was only when I really got to enjoy the game, and when I thought I might have a real chance at it. Only then I started to think about it as a career.
WJ: What else is there?

So what was your first big break?

LP: Getting a trial at Dagenham Damage. Can you believe that? (Luke shudders jokingly)
WJ: Audy McMahon spotted me playing for Essex.

Luke, you joined the Tigers as a youth player with Danny Rider. Are you still friends?

LP: Oh, yeah, but it's hard. They're at the other end of the country, you know. Run up a pretty hefty mobile bill... He was best man at my wedding, though.

Wes, have you had any problems with the ankle injury you sustained at the end of last season?

WJ: No, it's totally fine now.
LP: Yeah, just ask the Dagenham defence.
(They both laugh).

The ankle apart, you've both been lucky with injuries in your career. Has the ankle injury made you more aware of what can happen?

LP: Sure. But you can't afford to worry about it otherwise you'd hang off...
WJ: And you wouldn't go anywhere near Chopper, Grizz or Monk in training!

LP: I think training's essential to keep at the top of the game. I've learnt so much at the Comets already.
WJ: Luke always stays on to practise his free kicks for an hour at the end of the day.
LP: Just learning from the best. Cantona never stopped you know, and someone like Sampilson. Even our new lad, Zack Cassidy – he's always got a tennis ball on the go.
WJ: But injuries are our worst nightmares – you spend your whole life practising for something that can end in a moment. And our Physio "The Swede" is so scary. We'd do anything to avoid seeing The Swede... but I've had a chance to give the ankle all the rest it needs for now.

Any tips for the manager, Jim Carter?

LP: Anger management?
WJ: His golf swing needs a bit of work – pulls to the left...
LP: No, he's the best, you know. Hard, but at least he's unfair with it, you know...
(Both laughed).

Any predictions for where you might be in the League at the end of the season?

WJ: Only one place we belong.
LP: On the top, looking down. Same when we kick off for Europe next week.

Thanks fellas. ∎

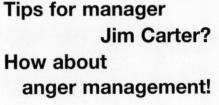

Tips for manager Jim Carter? How about anger management!

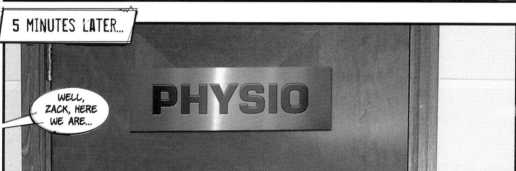

5 MINUTES LATER...

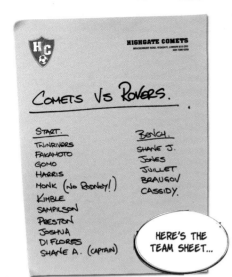

159

WELL, HERE WE GO, WITH WHAT COULD BE THE MINI CUP FINAL RIGHT HERE...

HEDGER

SURE ENOUGH THE ROYSTON ROVERS ARE TAKING AN ATTACKING LINE UP.

NEEDLING
WITH CHOPPER DAVIS

"GIVING YOUR OPPO 'THE NEEDLE' IS ALL PART OF THE GAME. NO MORE 'BEST OF LUCK' - IF YOU'RE TRYING TO STOP SOME 90 MILE AN HOUR WINGER, YOU'VE GOTTA TRY AND PUT 'EM OFF A BIT SO YOU MAKE A CRACK ABOUT THE MISSUS, THE HAIRCUT, WAY THEY WALK, CAR THEY DRIVE. DON'T GO TOO FAR, YOU DON'T WANT TO START A FIGHT, WELL, I TRY NOT TO. BUT SOME GUYS GET CARRIED AWAY.

AND HERE THEY COME...
...IT'S VAN DE KLAAS ONTO SAMPILSON.

165

GOAALLLLLLL!

ROYSTON ROVERS

HIGHGATE COMETS

2.0

AND KYLE... 2-0!

40 MINUTES...

IT'S FRANTIC DEFENDING HERE FROM THE 10-MAN COMETS SIDE...

THEY JUST CAN'T SEEM TO GET THE BALL AWAY!

HANG ON! DJ HAS CLEARED IT! ...TO ALAN SHANE...

WILMOT 6

ESPANA 10

OH, THIS IS SO QUICK! THE LINESMEN CAN'T KEEP UP!

WELL LAWRIE, WHAT ON EARTH DO YOU MAKE OF THAT?

BRING O
CASSI

DO YOU THINK THERE'S ANY CHANCE OF THEM PULLING ANY BACK?

MEANWHILE IN THE CHANGING ROOMS...

CAN'T GET THROUGH THE DEFENCE? CAN'T GET NEAR THE STINKIN' DEFENCE MORE LIKE! MAYBE IT'S JUST ME BUT I THINK WE'D HAVE A BETTER CHANCE OF SCORING IF THE BALL WAS IN THEIR PENALTY AREA NOT OURS!

...AND DO I HAVE A MIDFIELD? PRESTON, SAMPILSON, THEY'RE ALL OVER YOU! AS FOR YOU OTHER USELESS LUMPS, I CAN'T EVEN SEE YOU!!

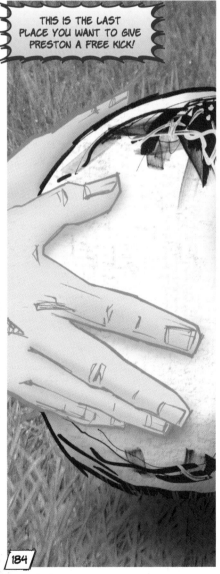

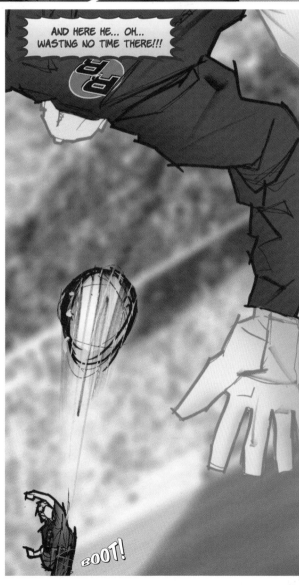

A BULLET OF A HEADER. GOAL, SHANE!

BOOM!

ABSOLUTELY BEAUTIFUL!!

GOAALLLLLLL!

CASSIDY... TO JOSHUA...

WES?

STILL JOSHUA...

HE'S DUMMIED! THE GOALIE'S DIVED!
IT'S IN, THEY'RE LEVEL!!!
3 ALL
I DON'T BELIEVE IT, TONY!!!

I DON'T BELIEVE IT!
CASSIDY FROM NOWHERE!!
HE SHOOTS!!!
CASSIDY
11
WHEEE

GOAAAL!!!!
AGGH!
NO... HANG ON, THE LINESMAN HAS HIS FLAG UP...
THE REF BLEW FOR THE FOUL ON PRESTON BEFORE CASSIDY... IT'S A PENALTY! WHAT DRAMA!
EEEEP!
NO...
THE REF'S CALLING NERO OVER...

HIGHGATE ECHO sport

4 AC

Rising star
4-3 come

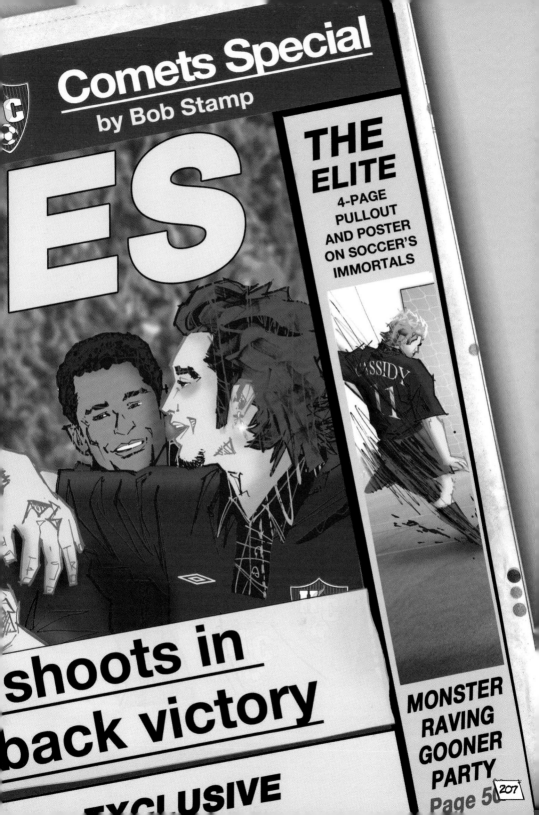